U0009848

附英語朗讀
QR Code

孩子的第一本
遊戲記憶&圖解
英語單字繪本

My First Book
of English Words

請連結至小熊出版網址
https://pse.is/LPQL6
或掃描 QR Code下載全
書音檔。

音檔下載連結

目次 Contents

The Alphabet
字母

Aa **Bb** **Cc** **Dd**

A / a   B / b   C / c   D / d

Hh **Ii** **Jj** **Kk**

H / h   I / i   J / j   K / k

Oo **Pp** **Qq** **Rr**

O / o   P / p   Q / q   R / r

Vv **Ww** **Xx**

V / v   W / w   X / x

Ee Ff Gg

E/e   F/f   G/g

Ll Mm Nn

L/l   M/m   N/n

Ss Tt Uu

S/s   T/t   U/u

Great!
真是太棒了！

Yy Zz

Y/y   Z/z

Greeting
問候

跟大家打招呼吧！

alarm clock
鬧鐘

bat
球棒

bed
床

blanket
毯子、被子

book
書

bookshelf
書櫃

box
箱子

My Room
我的房間

colored pencil
色鉛筆

coloring
著色

comic book
漫畫書

desk
書桌

doll
娃娃

dresser
梳妝臺

Earth
地球

toy
玩具

telescope
望遠鏡

sun
太陽

stuffed toy
填充玩具

star
星星

rocket
火箭

racket
球拍

puzzle
拼圖

game
遊戲

glove
手套

moon
月亮

picture
圖畫

picture book
圖畫書

pillow
枕頭

Clothes
服裝

gloves
手套

slippers
拖鞋

jacket
夾克、短外套

tie
領帶

cap
便帽、棒球帽

trousers
長褲

shirt
襯衫

hat
帽子

underpants
內褲

bag
袋子

T-shirt
T恤

dress
洋裝

skirt
裙子

socks
襪子

handkerchief
手帕

button
鈕扣

coat
外套、大衣

belt
腰帶

jeans
牛仔褲

pocket
口袋

raincoat
雨衣

sweater
毛衣

tights
緊身褲襪

shorts
短褲

scarf
圍巾、領巾

apron
圍裙

bowl
碗

broom
掃帚

cat
貓

cupboard
櫥櫃

dishcloth
擦碗巾

dustpan
畚箕

flower
花

Kitchen
廚房

frying pan
煎鍋

garbage box
垃圾桶

glass
玻璃杯

kettle
壺

kitchen timer
廚房計時器

whisk
攪拌器

toaster
烤麵包機

stove
爐子

sponge
海綿

sink
水槽

salt
鹽

rice cooker
電鍋

refrigerator
冰箱

microwave oven
微波爐

mixer
攪拌機、果汁機

mouse
老鼠

oven
烤箱

pepper
胡椒

pot
鍋、壺

13

apple
蘋果

bacon
培根

boiled egg
水煮蛋

bottle
瓶子

bread
麵包

butter
奶油

chair
椅子

chopsticks
筷子

Breakfast
早餐

coffee
咖啡

cup
杯子

dish
盤、碟

fork
叉子

fried egg
煎蛋

ham
火腿

honey
蜂蜜

yogurt
優格

toast
烤土司

tea
茶

table
桌子

sugar
糖

spoon
湯匙

soup
湯

jam
果醬

knife
刀子

milk
牛奶

pot
壺、鍋

salad
沙拉

sausage
香腸

My Family
我的家庭

grandmother
奶奶、外婆、(外)祖母

parents
父母

mother
媽媽

father
爸爸

sister
姊姊、妹妹

brother
哥哥、弟弟

16

grandfather
爺爺、外公、(外)祖父

uncle
叔叔、伯父
舅舅、姑丈

cousin
表(堂)兄弟姊妹

aunt
阿姨、姑姑
伯母、嬸嬸、舅媽

man
男人

woman
女人

boy
男孩

girl
女孩

baby
寶寶

air
conditioner
空調、冷暖氣機

curtain
窗簾

cushion
靠墊、坐墊

light
燈、光

newspaper
報紙

photo
照片

radio
收音機

Living Room
客廳

Entrance
玄關

rose
玫瑰

rug
地毯

sofa
沙發

TV
電視

window
窗戶

boots
靴子

doo
門

Yard
庭院

sunflower
向日葵

roof
屋頂

house
房子

garage
車庫

car
車

umbrella
傘

stamp
郵票

key
鑰匙

letter
信

sandals
涼鞋、拖鞋

shoes
鞋子

sneakers
運動鞋

stairs
樓梯

Bathroom
浴室

bathtub
浴缸

brush
刷子、鬃梳

bubble
泡泡

clean
乾淨的

comb
梳子

cotton
棉花

dirty
骯髒的

dry
乾的

fan
風扇

hair dryer
吹風機

hanger
衣架

mirror
鏡子

plug
塞子

razor
刮鬍刀

wet
溼的

water
水

washroom
洗手間

**washing
machine**
洗衣機

washbowl
臉盆

towel
毛巾

shampoo
洗髮精

shower
淋浴設備

soap
肥皂

toilet
馬桶

toothbrush
牙刷

toothpaste
牙膏

My Body
我的身體

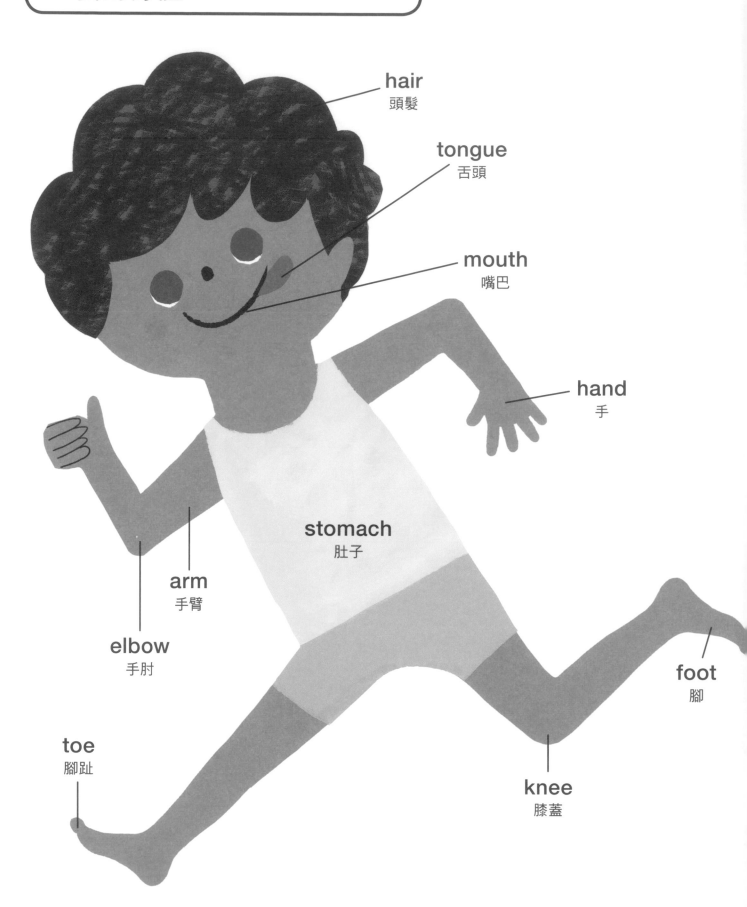

hair
頭髮

tongue
舌頭

mouth
嘴巴

hand
手

stomach
肚子

arm
手臂

elbow
手肘

toe
腳趾

knee
膝蓋

foot
腳

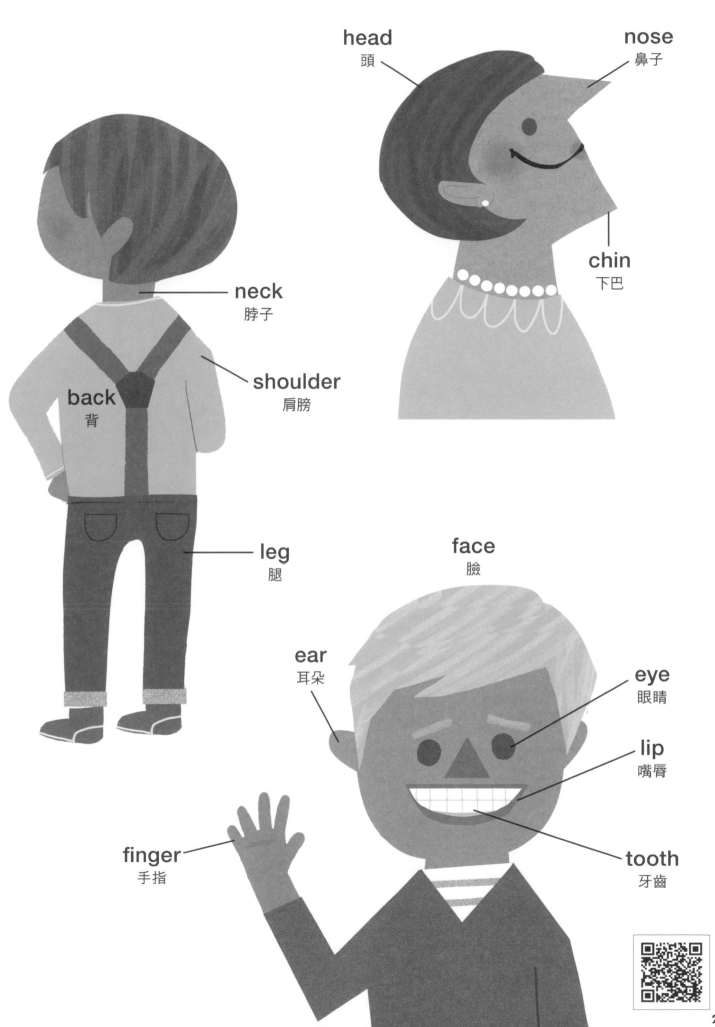

head
頭

nose
鼻子

chin
下巴

neck
脖子

shoulder
肩膀

back
背

leg
腿

face
臉

ear
耳朵

eye
眼睛

lip
嘴脣

tooth
牙齒

finger
手指

blackboard
黑板

chalk
粉筆

classroom
教室

clock
時鐘

computer
電腦

dictionary
字典

English
英語

eraser
橡皮擦

School
學校

friend
朋友

geography
地理

globe
地球儀

history
歷史

Mandarin
國語

keyboard
鍵盤

map
地圖

math
數學

English

math

science

P.E

Mandarin

social studies

geography

history

triangle
三角形

teacher
老師

study
學習、研讀

student
學生

stapler
釘書機

square
正方形

social studies
社會

science
科學

microscope
顯微鏡

notebook
筆記本

paper
紙

P.E.
體育

pen
筆

pencil
鉛筆

ruler
尺

castanet
響板

drum
鼓

guitar
吉他

piano
鋼琴

recorder
直笛

song
歌曲

tambourine
鈴鼓

Music
音樂

violin
小提琴

black
黑色

blue
藍色

brown
棕色、褐色

brush
筆刷、畫筆

clay
黏土

Art
藝術

yellow
黃色

white
白色

silver
銀色

scissors
剪刀

red
紅色

purple
紫色

pink
粉紅色

paint
顏料

color
顏色

crayon
蠟筆

glue
膠水

gold
金色

gray
灰色

green
綠色

27

Sports
運動

marathon
馬拉松

baseball
棒球

soccer
足球

golf
高爾夫球

rugby
（英式）橄欖球

tennis
網球

skiing
滑雪

surfing
衝浪

table tennis
桌球

karate
空手道

volleyball
排球

ballet
芭蕾

sumo
wrestling
相撲

basketball
籃球

badminton
羽球

dodgeball
躲避球

wrestling
角力

skating
滑冰

swimming
游泳

ant
螞蟻

ball
球

bee
蜜蜂

bench
長凳

bicycle
腳踏車

bird
鳥

boat
小船

butterfly
蝴蝶

child
小孩

Park
公園

dandelion
蒲公英

dog
狗

duck
鴨

fountain
噴水池

frog
青蛙

grasshopper
蚱蜢

jumping rope
跳繩

kite
風箏

tricycle
三輪車

tree
樹

swing
盪秋千

squirrel
松鼠

spider
蜘蛛

sparrow
麻雀

snake
蛇

snail
蝸牛

 eaf
葉

 nest
巢

 pigeon
鴿子

pond
池塘

 **seesaw**
翹翹板

 slide
滑梯

 smart phone
智慧型手機

airplane
飛機

airport
機場

ambulance
救護車

bank
銀行

bridge
橋

bus
公車

bus stop
公車站

convenience
store
便利商店

Town
城鎮

department
store
百貨公司

driver
司機、駕駛

fire engine
消防車

fire station
消防局

flower shop
花店

helicopter
直升機

hotel
旅館

truck
卡車

train
火車

traffic light
交通號誌燈

taxi
計程車

station
車站

road
道路

post office
郵局

police station
警察局

police car
警車

library
圖書館

mailbox
郵筒

motorcycle
摩托車

movie theater
電影院

museum
博物館

parking lot
停車場

33

Conversation 會話
（問路／購物）

你能說明路線嗎？

你能用英語購物嗎？

How much is it?
這個東西多少錢？

It is $100.
這個一百元。

Jobs
工作

astronaut
太空人

singer
歌手

pastry chef
糕點師

doctor
醫師

nurse
護理師

vet
獸醫師

police
officer
警察

dentist
牙醫師

fire fighter
消防員

fisherman
漁夫

lawyer
律師

actor
演員

flight
attendant
空服員

painter
畫家

baseball
player
棒球選手

dancer
舞蹈家

soccer
player
足球選手

office
worker
上班族

florist
花匠

baker
麵包師傅

farmer
農夫

Supermarket
超市

beef
牛肉

cabbage
甘藍

can
罐頭

carrot
胡蘿蔔

cart
手推車

chicken
雞肉

corn
玉米

cucumber
黃瓜

egg
蛋

fish
魚

food
食物

fruit
水果

garlic
大蒜

lemon
檸檬

lettuce
萵苣

vegetable
蔬菜

tuna
鮪魚

tomato
番茄

toilet paper
衛生紙

shopping basket
購物籃

salmon
鮭魚

pumpkin
南瓜

fruit

1

2

meat
肉

melon
甜瓜、哈密瓜

money
錢

onion
洋蔥

peach
水蜜桃

pork
豬肉

potato
馬鈴薯

bear
熊

chimpanzee
黑猩猩

crocodile
短吻鱷

deer
鹿

dolphin
海豚

elephant
大象

flamingo
紅鶴

Zoo／Animals
動物園／動物

Aquarium
水族館

fox
狐狸

giraffe
長頸鹿

gorilla
大猩猩

jellyfish
水母

kangaroo
袋鼠

koala
無尾熊

leopard
豹

zebra
斑馬

wolf
狼

turtle
龜

tiger
老虎

shark
鯊魚

seal
海豹

raccoon dog
貉

lion
獅子

monkey
猴子

panda
貓熊

parrot
鸚鵡

penguin
企鵝

polar bear
北極熊

41

Vacation
假期

camping
露營

cow
乳牛

fishing
釣魚

hill
小丘、丘陵

horse
馬

lunch
午餐

mountain
山

pig
豬

rabbit
兔子

rice ball
飯糰

river
河川

rock
岩石

sheep
綿羊

tent
帳篷

water bott
水壺

waves
波浪

swimsuit
泳衣

sunglasses
太陽眼鏡

starfish
海星

sky
天空

ship
船

seashell
貝殼

waterfall
瀑布

beach
海灘

bucket
水桶

crab
蟹

island
島

sand
沙

sea
海

43

balloon
氣球

cake
蛋糕

camera
相機

candle
蠟燭

candy
糖果

cherry
櫻桃

chocolate
巧克力

Party
派對

Happy

cookie
餅乾

donut
甜甜圈

French fries
薯條

fried chicken
炸雞

grapes
葡萄

Happy birthday

happy birthday
生日快樂

irthday

strawberry
草莓

straw
吸管

sandwiches
三明治

ribbon
緞帶

pudding
布丁

present
禮物

potato chips
洋芋片

ice cream
冰淇淋

juice
果汁

magic
魔術

pizza
披薩

popcorn
爆米花

Restaurant
餐廳

banana
香蕉

beer
啤酒

cheese
起司

chef
主廚

curry and rice
咖哩飯

delicious
美味的

dessert
甜點

dinner
晚餐

drink
飲料、喝

fried shrimp
炸蝦

fry
炸

grilled fish
烤魚

hamburg
漢堡（肉）

wine
酒

waitress
服務生（女）

waiter
服務生（男）

tray
托盤

steak
牛排

soda
汽水

rice
米飯

menu
菜單

noodle
麵

omelet
蛋包飯

orange
柑橘、柳橙

pancake
薄煎餅、鬆餅

pasta
義大利麵、通心麵

Conversation 會話（點餐）

到餐廳點餐吧！

Here you are.
這是你的餐點。

Thank you.
謝謝你。

My Day 我的一天

I wake up.
我起床了。

I wash my face.
我在洗臉。

I make my bed.
我在整理床鋪。

I have breakfast.
我在吃早餐。

I check my school bag.
我在整理書包。

I leave my house.
我出門了。

I take out the garbage.
我去倒垃圾。

I go to school.
我去上學。

I have lunch.
我在吃午餐。

I study science.
我在研究科學。

I play soccer.
我在踢足球。

I go home.
我回家了。

I do my homework.
我在寫作業。

I have dinner.
我在吃晚餐。

I watch TV.
我在看電視。

I take a bath.
我在洗澡。

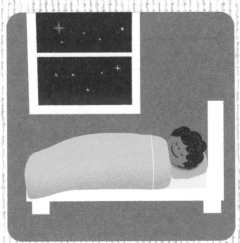

I go to bed.
我去睡覺了。

Good night.
晚安。

Doing Things
活動

play
玩

listen to
聽

dance
跳舞

wash
清洗

sit down
坐下

stand up
起立

cut
切

swim
游泳

draw
繪畫

look at
看

touch
摸

jump
跳

sleep
睡覺

cook 烹調、料理

boil 烹煮、煮沸

turn 轉、旋轉

buy 購買

talk 談話

eat 吃

walk 走

throw 投、擲、拋

ride 騎

make 製作

write 書寫

sing 演唱

run 跑

kick 踢

laugh 笑

cry 哭

open 打開、翻開

Opposite Words 相反詞

front 前面

back 後面

cold 冷的 hot 熱的

left 左邊

old 舊的 new 新的

big 大的

small 小的

bad 壞的 good 好的

short 短的

Feelings 心情

angry 生氣的

happy 開心的

shy 害羞的

funny 好笑的

scared 害怕的

brave 勇敢的

sad 悲傷的

relaxed 放鬆的

right 右邊

fast 快的

slow 慢的

few 少量的

many 大量的

hard 硬的

soft 軟的

light 輕的

high 高的

heavy 重的

low 低的

long 長的

 **proud** 驕傲的

 **worried** 擔憂的

 **surprised** 驚訝的

 **bored** 無聊的

 **tired** 疲累的

hungry 飢餓的

 **thirsty** 口渴的

Numbers
數字

0	zero	
1	one	
2	two	
3	three	
4	four	
5	five	
6	six	
7	seven	
8	eight	
9	nine	
10	ten	
11	eleven	
12	twelve	
13	thirteen	
14	fourteen	
15	fifteen	
16	sixteen	
17	seventeen	
18	eighteen	
19	nineteen	
20	twenty	

2
second
第二

1
first
第一

3
third
第三

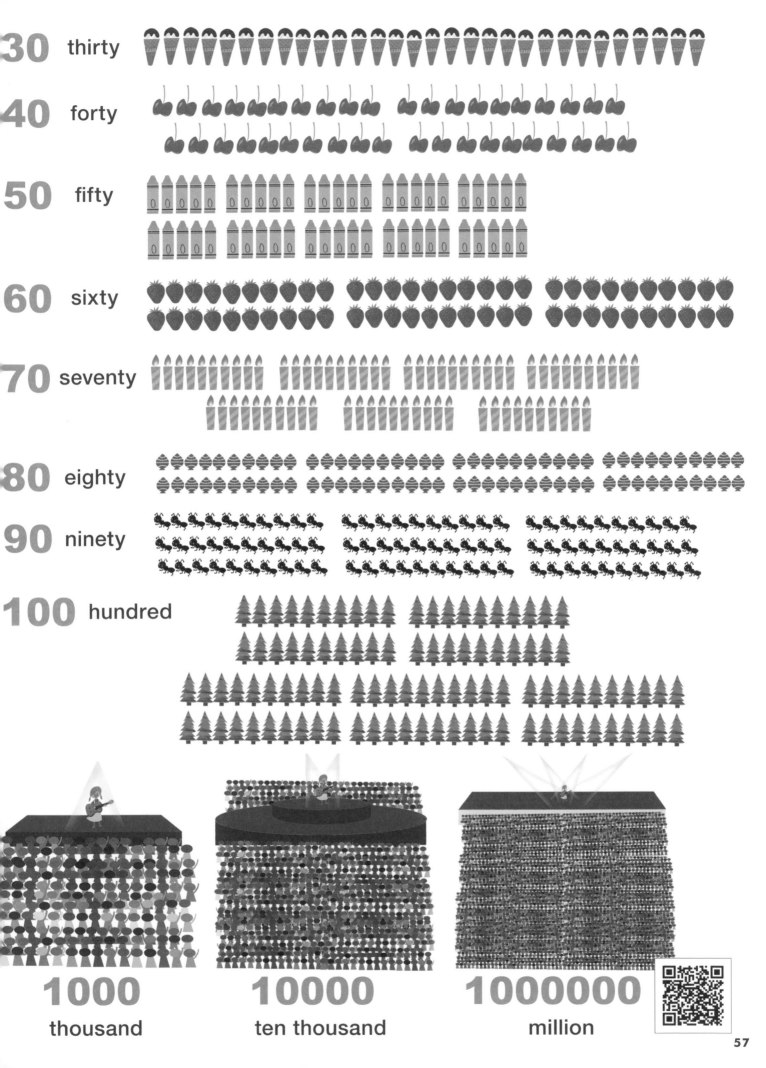

30 thirty

40 forty

50 fifty

60 sixty

70 seventy

80 eighty

90 ninety

100 hundred

1000 thousand

10000 ten thousand

1000000 million

Months 月份

year
年

January
一月

February
二月

March
三月

April
四月

May
五月

June
六月

July
七月

August
八月

September
九月

October
十月

November
十一月

December
十二月

spring
春

summer
夏

season
季節

winter
冬

fall
秋

58

A Week 一星期

星期一
Monday

星期二
Tuesday

星期三
Wednesday

星期四
Thursday

星期五
Friday

星期六
Saturday

星期日
Sunday

time 時間

 6 o'clock 6點鐘

 12 o'clock 12點鐘

 8 o'clock 8點鐘

morning 早上

afternoon 中午

night 晚上

Weather 天氣

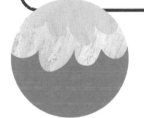
cloudy 多雲的

sunny 晴朗的

rainy 多雨的

cloud 雲

rainbow 彩虹

snow 雪

wind 風

thunder 雷

storm 暴風雨

Country
國家

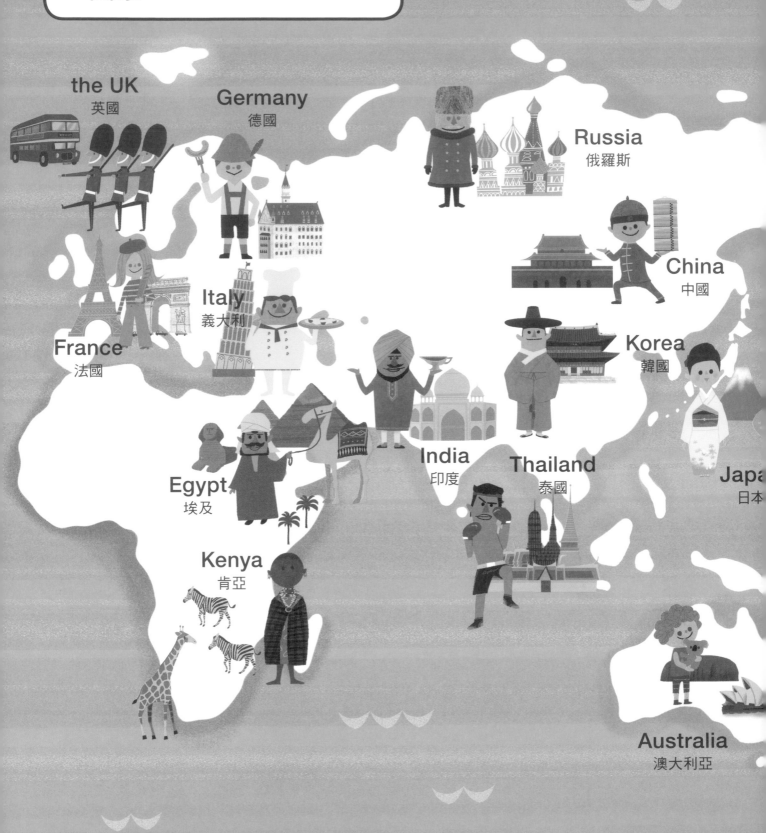

the UK
英國

Germany
德國

Russia
俄羅斯

China
中國

France
法國

Italy
義大利

Korea
韓國

Egypt
埃及

India
印度

Thailand
泰國

Japa
日本

Kenya
肯亞

Australia
澳大利亞

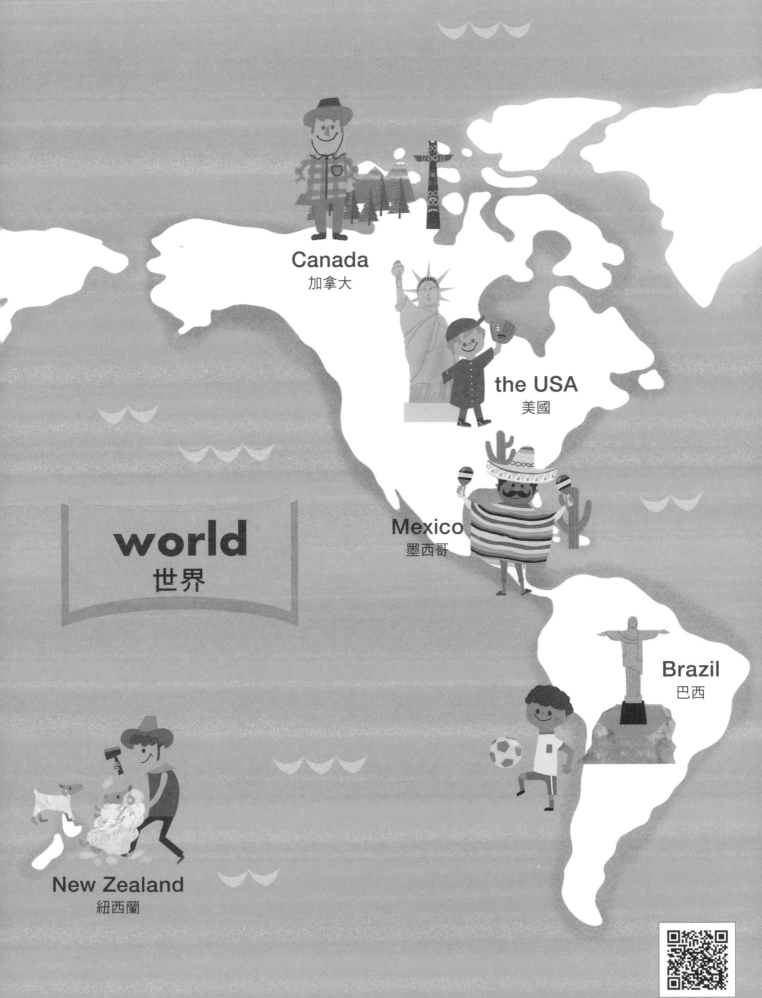

world
世界

Canada
加拿大

the USA
美國

Mexico
墨西哥

Brazil
巴西

New Zealand
紐西蘭

Conversation 會話

你有想去旅行的國家嗎？

Where do you want to go?

你想去哪裡？

I want to go to France.

我想去法國。

下次再一起玩吧！

Index 索引

監修／Allen 玉井光江

出生於日本廣島縣。美國加利福尼亞州那慕爾聖母大學英語學系畢業，舊金山州立大學英語學研究所碩士、天普大學教育學研究所博士。現為日本青山大學外語學院英語學系教授、日本兒童英語教育學會理事。

繪圖／手塚明美

1967年出生於日本神奈川縣，在橫濱長大。曾任職視覺設計公司，於1998年起擔任自由接案插畫家。作品包括與語言學習相關的書籍、雜誌插畫，現為日本兒童出版美術家聯盟會員，興趣是帶狗散步，居住在東京。

翻譯／陳潔

國立臺灣師範大學畢業，曾任教科書、童書、知識漫畫書編輯，喜歡關注語言學習、人文史地與社會科學議題，熱愛文字與藝術創作。

推薦閱讀

孩子的第一本 情境學習英語繪本

看繪本，聽CD，學英語！圖繪日常生活情境，活用超過250句簡單句型，讓孩子在生活中，自然而然開口說英語，快樂踏出英語學習的第一步！

監修：外山節子 | 繪圖：手塚明美 | 翻譯：林劭貞 | 精裝 | 21.4 x 28.4 cm | 48頁

英語學習

孩子的第一本遊戲記憶&圖解英語單字繪本
My First Book of English Words：Find & Memorize!

監修：Allen 玉井光江 | 繪圖：手塚明美 | 翻譯：陳潔

英語朗讀：下薰（Magical Kids 英語研究所）| 設計：公平惠美
聲音錄製：MEDIASTYLIST 股份公司 | 編輯協力：マキモトユキコ、久保庭友紀子

總編輯：鄭如瑤 | 責任編輯：陳怡潔 | 美術編輯：莊芯媚
行銷主任：塗幸儀 | 錄音：印笛錄音製作有限公司
社長：郭重興 | 發行人兼出版總監：曾大福
業務平臺總經理：李雪麗 | 業務平臺副總經理：李復民 | 實體通路協理：林詩富
網路暨海外通路協理：張鑫峰 | 特販通路協理：陳綺瑩 | 印務經理：黃禮賢
出版與發行：小熊出版・遠足文化事業股份有限公司 | 地址：231 新北市新店區民權路 108-2 號 9 樓
電話：02-22181417 | 傳真：02-86671851 | 客服專線：0800-221029
劃撥帳號：19504465 | 戶名：遠足文化事業股份有限公司
Facebook：小熊出版 | E-mail：littlebear@bookrep.com.tw
讀書共和國出版集團客服信箱：service@bookrep.com.tw
讀書共和國出版集團網路書店：http://www.bookrep.com.tw
團體訂購請洽業務部：02-22181417 分機 1132、1520
法律顧問：華洋法律事務所／蘇文生律師 | 印製：凱林彩印股份有限公司
初版一刷：2019 年 12 月 | 初版二刷：2020 年 2 月
定價：380 元 | ISBN：978-986-5503-12-3

版權所有・翻印必究　缺頁或破損請寄回更換
特別聲明　有關本書中的言論內容，不代表本公司／出版集團之立場與意見，文責由作者自行承擔

國家圖書館出版品預行編目 (CIP) 資料

孩子的第一本遊戲記憶&圖解英語單字繪本 / Allen 玉井光江監修；手塚明美繪；陳 潔譯 . -- 初版 . -- 新北市：小熊出版：遠足文化發行 , 2019.12
72 面；21.6×28.9 公分 . -- (英語學習)
譯自：はじめてのさがしておぼえるえいごのことば
ISBN 978-986-5503-12-3 (精裝)

1. 英語　2. 詞彙

805.12　　　　　　　　　　　108018049

小熊出版官方網頁　　小熊出版讀者回函